THE LOVE SONG OF MONKEY

THE LOVE SONG
OF
MONKEY

A Novel

Michael S.A. Graziano

Leapfrog Press
Teaticket, Massachusetts

Published in 2008 in the United States by
Leapfrog Press LLC
PO Box 2110
Teaticket, MA 02536
www.leapfrogpress.com

Distributed in the United States by
Consortium Book Sales and Distribution
St. Paul, Minnesota 55114
www.cbsd.com

First Edition

Library of Congress Cataloging-in-Publication Data

Graziano, Michael S. A., 1967-
  The love song of monkey / Michael S.A. Graziano.
    p. cm.
  ISBN 978-0-9815148-0-2
  1. AIDS (Disease)–Patients–Fiction. 2. AIDS (Disease)–Alterna-
tive treatment–Fiction. 3. Triangles (Interpersonal relations)–
Fiction. I. Title.
  PS3607.R39935L68 2008
  813'.6–dc22

    2008014723

Printed in the United States of America

For C., C., and M.

Let us go then, you and I,
When the evening is spread out against the sky
Like a patient etherized upon a table;
Let us go, through certain half-deserted streets,
The muttering retreats
Of restless nights in one-night cheap hotels
And sawdust restaurants with oyster-shells:
Streets that follow like a tedious argument
Of insidious intent
To lead you to an overwhelming question. . . .
Oh, do not ask, "What is it?"
Let us go and make our visit.

—T. S. Eliot, *The Love Song of J. Alfred Prufrock*

PART I

1

Kitty drove me to the hospital at two in the morning. I sat in the back seat so that I could lie down if I wanted to. I didn't put on my seat belt because I didn't like the way it pinched me around the middle. I had a blanket pulled around me, tented around my shoulders, and the blue fuzz from the blanket kept snagging on my facial stubble. I hadn't shaved in two days and Kitty said that my face was growing Velcro. Everything stuck to it. Blankets, socks, bits of lint and tissue.

I had not been outside in weeks so I stared curiously out of the car window at the streets and buildings passing by. I felt like a ghost, white-faced, looking at a world I used to belong to. The people were so far away that they didn't bother me. They were like people on a fuzzy black-and-white TV screen. I was surprised at how crowded the streets were, how many people were out in the middle of the night, walking in groups, flagging down taxis, even some of them still working.

I saw a pizza deliveryman with six boxes of pizza strapped to the back of his bicycle. All of a sudden I could taste pepperoni, and I had a longing for pizza.

I saw a construction crew in yellow boots working on a hole in the street with blazing bright electric lights shining down on them. The lights were so bright that they sent a pain stabbing through my head as we passed, and I cringed and closed my eyes.

"Sorry about that," Kitty said. "Sorry, I couldn't help that."

Kitty was a nervous person. She was a flibbertigibbet. Professionally she was an art critic, but personally she was a flibbertigibbet. Even before I got sick, she was always in a flutter. Every word she said sounded like a reflex jerked out of her. As she drove, her head turned nervously from side to side and I could see two cords standing out on the back of her neck. She made little clicking, muttering noises to herself about the other drivers or about the way to the hospital. She was always narrating her life under her breath.

When we reached the hospital we had to stop on the ramp leading to the parking garage while a security guard checked us over. Kitty opened the window on her side and looked up at him out of her frizz of blond hair that always looked like an electric halo around her face, and the guard leaned close and peered tiredly down at her. He had a flashlight in his hand but he didn't shine it in at us. He had a little fragment of potato chip stuck to his lip.

A wave of cold struck into the car through the open window and I hated that guard. Couldn't he see there was a patient in the back seat? I shrank into the blanket and glared at him. It was probably warm out; it was spring, late April, and the people on the streets were dressed in light jackets; but I was too sick to appreciate the spring air.

The guard didn't say anything. After a moment of peering into the car he started chewing his mouthful of potato chips again, nodded tiredly, and waved us through with his flashlight. Kitty closed the window and nosed up the ramp into the parking garage.

We found a spot on the first level only a few yards from the hospital entrance. Kitty got out, opened the car door on my side, and an oily reek surrounded me and stuck in my throat.

"Are you ready?" she said anxiously. "Can you walk okay? How's your feet? Do you want to lean on me? It's not far. It's just to the door there, see, it'll take half a minute, is that okay? Are you okay?"

Ever since I had gotten sick I had more or less stopped talking. It cost too much energy to marshal up the words. Kitty usually tried to keep up a stream of anxious chatter to fill in the silence.

She helped me out of the car and I stood with the blanket wrapped tightly around my shoulders. My legs and feet were icy cold below the cuffs of my jeans. I was barefoot; I couldn't wear shoes. My feet had sores on them where the skin had pulled too tight over the bones.

"You can do it," Kitty said, leading me toward the glass door, her shoes scraping and clattering on the cement, echoing in the nighttime quiet. "It's only a few steps." We walked slowly, her arm around me. When we reached the door it slid open automatically. Inside, the bright light made me cringe as if somebody had hit me in the face. The air was dry, sterile, colder than the outside air, and the floor was like polished ice on my damaged feet. We were in a narrow room with a row of pink plastic chairs along one wall and a welcome desk at the other end.

The receptionist got up from behind the desk and came toward us. He was about my height but much fatter. I was so used to looking at Kitty or at myself in a mirror that I had forgotten how fleshy other people generally were. He had a fatuous smile on his white fleshy face. His two plump hands were clasped together like lumps of dough. He was wearing blue hospital scrubs, white new sneakers, and a white coat with a nametag. His name was Earl.

"And which one of you is sick today?" he said.

He probably meant it innocently, and maybe he

said it to every couple that came in the door. But Kitty gave a nervous gasp and stepped back, staring at him with her eyes open in an astonished outrage. She was anorexic and looked almost as wasted and sick as I did. She didn't like to be reminded of it and was shocked when anyone mentioned it to her.

"My husband," she said, stiffly, "is here to see Dr. Kack."

"Wonderful," the receptionist said, his smile undented. "But your husband can't come in without shoes. Didn't you bring shoes?"

"He doesn't wear shoes," Kitty said.

"He can't walk in here without shoes. We'll have to put him in slippers."

"No," Kitty said, glancing at me nervously. "He doesn't wear anything on his feet. He can't. It hurts too much." She glared at the receptionist and I felt proud of her. Whatever trouble we may have had in private, we kept up a united front in public. She was ready to do battle for me. A certain hysterical ferocity was taking shape in her expression, in her pinched face and pointed chin.

The receptionist smiled at her, then turned and smiled at me, and then suddenly said, "Wonderful, we'll find a wheelchair and he can put his feet up on the footrests. We can't have bare feet treading over the hospital floors."

"Thank you," Kitty said, shrilly, with dislike in her

voice. "That will be fine. Can you take us to see Dr. Kack? He knows that we're coming. I called him half an hour ago."

She was furious now, because Dr. Kack had warned us to keep the visit a strict secret and in her usual manner she had blown the secret already.

2

I sat in the wheelchair shivering, my blanket wrapped around me to the chin and my thin starved-looking feet shaking on the metal footrests. Kitty wheeled me down the corridor and I could hear the pistol shots of her heels on the hard floor. We went down the elevator to the lowest basement, where the laboratories were. It was four stories below ground level, and very quiet.

"You're late," Dr. Kack said, frowning out of his laboratory door. He strode toward us with a lanky movement, forcefully took hold of the wheelchair handles, and wheeled me in the door backward. My head spun from the motion.

I had never met him; Kitty knew him. He was a tall man, probably in his forties, dark hair in a horseshoe and a slightly dented bald forehead. I had the absurd but compelling impression that he must have spent so much time thinking with his forehead in his hands that he had left thumbprints on it, and that was why his forehead was dented at the sides. He had a thin face, pinched and lined, and an intensity to his eyes, an impatience and a roving quickness magnified through very large glasses. He was wearing a dark suit and tie and brown penny loafers without the pennies; but the clothes didn't fit him somehow; he looked as if he might be more comfortable in beach clothes.

The room did not look like a laboratory. It looked like a cocktail lounge, with stylish black leather couches and expensive wooden lamps and a fake palm plant. It was a depressing room, actually, and obviously a lie. It seemed to say, "Please make yourself comfortable while we tell you that you're about to die."

Kitty sat down nervously with a fluttering smile. Dr. Kack sat on the couch across from us and leaned forward eagerly, staring at me, his long boney hands trembling slightly on his knees. I could see he wasn't angry or annoyed that we were late; but he was impatient. He had a gloating expression that he did not even try to hide.

"Right," he said. "Right." He had a nervous gesture of lifting his hand as if to straighten his glasses, pausing with his fingers curved into a grip an inch from the frames, and then changing his mind and putting his hand swiftly down again. "We better get this understood at the beginning. Let's put it simply. You have a certain disease."

I nodded.

He looked at me shrewdly. Kitty must have told him about me, spilling her guts to him, and he would have guessed pretty close to the truth. He didn't say anything about my tantrums or my mood swings or my having flushed all the pills down the toilet in a rage the other day. I'm sure Kitty had described it in detail, but he didn't say a word about it. He glanced at Kitty. "How much did you tell him about the project?"

She smiled nervously. "I told him what you wanted me to."

"Right," he said. "Right. You have a disease. I might have a cure. It's a tremendous thing. Sadly, given the current regulatory climate, there's no way I can get approval for phase 1 trials. I won't even submit the proposal, not at this point. Do you *know* the kinds of hurdles they. . . ."

He stopped himself on the brink of what looked like a regular diatribe, choking back the agitation and frustration in his voice. He laughed, almost a giggle, his eyes opening wide, his hands spreading out.

"Right. Here's what I mean to say. I have a cure, but admittedly it has a certain propensity to kill rats and other lab animals. I'll give you a crack at getting cured, you give me a human test subject, and the agreement is that nothing ever gets said to anybody.

ANYbody." He smiled pleasantly, folded his hands together over his stomach, and sat back in his chair. "Are we all happy?"

3

Kack brought to my mind Kalculation. His mind always on his work, forever improving his invention. Wheels and gears and diodes and transistors in his head. I could see all these things in his eyes. He knew more than he was willing to say. He didn't want to ask me any awkward details because he wanted me as a subject. All his heart was set on me, on putting me through his invention.

For my part, I was willing. I felt reckless. Here was as good a way to commit suicide as any. I liked him from the start because of his originality and his flair. Besides, the three of us together were so preposterous that I was entertained for the first time in weeks and started to grin. We were all three gaunt, our faces drawn, our eyes flashing uneasily and nervously at each other. If Earl from the welcome booth had looked in at that moment he might have scratched his head and wondered which one of us was sick today.

"Tell me about the cure, Dr.," I said. Kitty was

shocked to hear me speak up. She stared at me, her mouth popping open. Maybe getting out of my room had done me some good after all; I felt that my mind was freshened up somehow and I was curious again.

"I mean to tell you everything," Dr. Kack said. "I need you to understand. Without that, without you trying your hardest, we won't go anywhere. Are you good at taking pain?"

Kitty gave a little jump as if someone had stuck her with a pin and said, "You didn't say anything about pain. You didn't tell me that. It's going to hurt him?"

Dr. Kack stirred uneasily. "Like I said, I mean to tell you everything."

I grinned again. Pain seemed unimportant to me at that moment. "Tell me all the details," I said.

Dr. Kack lifted his hand to his glasses, paused, thought carefully, and then launched into his explanation, which sounded like a speech he must have given already to a room full of imaginary investors. He obviously didn't often get the chance to spew it out to an actual person, and since I sat quietly, attentively watching his face, nodding at the right moments, he seemed encouraged and his enthusiasm blossomed. His long fingers moved and shaped around his ideas. I felt a kinship with him; he was as obsessed as I was in his own way, and I appreciated that.

"What is medicine? Honestly? A witch doctor, he waves his feather duster over your head. He works at the spirit level. In fact, he works at the placebo level, which is powerful and works extremely well. This is a psychological level of intervention. So far so good. But medicine progresses. A battle surgeon. You break a bone, he sets it. You get a spear to the side, he binds the wound together. This is a mechanical intervention. This is the body as tubes and struts. Excellent. If the spear doesn't go in too far, you are okay. But the march of progress continues. The next level that medicine reaches? In the nineteenth century, microscopic germs. Kill them, soap them, sterilize them. In the early twentieth century, douse them in antibiotics. But how do the antibiotics work? There we go deeper. There we reach the molecular level. You see, don't you, that the medicine of the twentieth century was obsessed with molecular intervention? Fix the break at the level of enzymes, of proteins, even DNA. But me, I am a physicist. I want to think as far down that path as possible. What follows logically after the molecular level? Atomic? Can you build a machine that fixes a broken arrangement of carbon atoms? Polish the membrane of a cell? Fix broken bones in the cytoskeleton, *inside* the cell? Can you go further, repair the arrangement of electrons and nucleons? Oh, I am an obsessive, I know. What about the level of quarks and gluons? I am talking about medicine at the level of quarks. Quarks. Do you get it? My machine can scan the structure of your cells, their scaffolding, molecules, atoms, down to the quark, and fix the breaks, regularize the lattice, put in place levees and dams, cure you, safeguard you, and make you unbreakable. How can I put anesthetics into your blood during a process like that? The machine would regularize you, turn you into a perfect, forever anesthetized person. No, the drug is unworkable. We need to strap you to the table awake, keep you as still as we can, and the machine reads you and fixes you and there's no alternative. You take the pain."

"This is actually possible?" I said.

"Of course it's possible," he said, testily. "I built it. I have a patent pending, and I've trademarked Kwark-King, Mr. Kwark, and Dr. Kack's Pimple Remover. Because it would, you know. It would cure a pimple. If you can take the pain."

"How much pain?" I said. "Have you tried it?"

"Me?" he said, incensed. "Don't be stupid. I give you a rubber squeeze bulb in your right hand. Are you right handed? And if the pain gets too much, you squeeze the bulb and the machine shuts down. It's that simple. It's up to you. If you are a hundred percent in it, then we can get pretty far. If you quit early, then. . . ." He shrugged and spread out his hands.

4

"You're not the first patient," he said. "Don't think I'm desperate." I was pretty sure that he *was* desperate, but I didn't interrupt. "I've had two others. The first one, we put him in a prototype machine. Kwark-King 1.2. We're now at 5.7. He had corns. Terrible corns on his feet, mainly his left foot. This was my sister's father-in-law. Anyway, he said he'd give it a whirl, if it'd get rid of the corns, so we strapped him in, and we turned it on. That was last year. It was very exciting."

"What happened?" I said.

"Well." Dr. Kack shrugged, with half a smile. "He gave an almighty yell and squeezed the bulb as fast as he could. It was just a prototype, remember. He thought I had lit his foot on fire. Stupid fool. He wanted to sue me at first."

"But what happened to his corns?"

"That's just it. He saw his corns, took one look, and he thanked me. He stopped all that talk about a lawsuit. Thank goodness his reaction time was slow. The beam worked up from the bottom of his left foot and reached about two millimeters into the skin before he was able to turn it off. It more or less took out his corns. The bottom of his left foot is as smooth and perfect and healthy as youth. Medically very strange. I'd like to see the look on his podiatrist's face. A patch of healthy, unblemished growth in the middle of that wrinkled up old man's foot. We cured his corns all right. I asked him if he wanted the other foot done, but he said no. Not for a million dollars, I think, is the exact phrase. The pain was too much for him. I'm not telling you this to put you off. Understand why I'm telling you. That man had a chance to rejuvenate from toe to head. He had a chance at perfect health. An hour of pain, and after that, a hundred years, two hundred years? A thousand? There is no basis for knowing. Once the subatomic lattice is set right, blemishes removed, the parts made to interlock optimally, it becomes immensely durable. But it takes someone of a certain mental strength. Kitty's told me a little about you and I have hopes for you. I think you have a kind of toughness. I think you're the one."

"Thanks," I said dryly, aware that he was trying to convince me through flattery. "But I'd like to know what happened to the second patient."

"Yes," he said. "Right. The second patient. The. . . . Again, it's a matter of mental strength. I should never have let him try. Poor man had bladder cancer, very poor prognosis, essentially untreatable. A friend of a friend, you understand. Very low morale. Very weak psychologically. We gave him a try, and at first I thought he was taking the pain well. The beam had progressed all the way up to the ankle bone. About two inches. About a minute and a half. I was excited, I can tell you. But the pain may have caused some psychological shock that prevented him from reacting at first. After a minute and thirty-two seconds he terminated the sequence and lay there screaming. That's all we ever got out of him. Screaming. His cancer did him in a week later. But I'll tell you this. If we ever dig up his coffin, we'll find both his feet in perfect shape, up to the ankle bone. Forever more. I'm telling you, this is new. This is revolutionary. What I want is a pioneer. Someone who can grasp the benefits and who can stick it out. Someone who can take my machine on a real honest-to-god spin around the block. That's why I need you to know what to expect ahead of time, so that you don't turn it off at the first shock. Forewarned, so they tell me, is forearmed."

5

Kitty sat muttering to herself, gasping now and then as if privately shocked or outraged by this or that comment, shifting in her seat, occasionally lifting her thin claw a few inches from her lap as if she thought she was still in school and was about to raise her hand to ask a question. Finally she couldn't keep her agitation contained any longer and blurted out, "Richard, you didn't tell me any of this. It sounds awful. He can't go through that. No. He can't. Richard why can't you test a rat or a . . . a rabbit, or whatever you test? You didn't tell me about how much it hurts."

"But I'm telling you now," he said, impatiently. "Of course, if you don't want to risk it, you can go home again and trust your luck with AIDS. I'm not stopping you. Go ahead." He glared at us fiercely out of his thick glasses. Kitty stared back at him with her mouth partly open, as if all her words had been knocked out of her lungs by his pugnacious reply. She looked on the verge of tears.

"There's no reason to get angry," I said. "It's a reasonable question. Why can't you test a squirrel instead of a person?"

"Don't think I haven't," he said. "I'm not an idiot. I'm a scientist. You don't know how many mice and cats and iguanas have gone through that machine. But it doesn't work. A cat can't tell you afterward what the experience was like. A cat can't regulate its response to pain. I strap in a cat and run the machine, and the beam passes over the entire body, tail to head. It takes about twenty minutes. I run a second beam to catch the errors of the first pass. Then I turn off the machine and take out the cat. And the cat is dead. I think the pain, the nerve stimulation, is so extreme that the animal can't comprehend and can't withstand the experience. It goes into a permanent torpor. The cells are still alive, the heart is beating, and the animal is mentally dead. Every animal I've tried descends into a permanent coma. But a human, that is fundamentally different. A human has the capacity to understand, the mental strength to resist, and the option of terminating the sequence. My belief is that a human with the required strength of mind could get very far through the sequence. That's what I'm hoping."

"But if he can only take it up to his ankles," Kitty said shrilly, "what good does that do him? His ankles are cured of AIDS?"

Dr. Kack shrugged and spread out his hands. "That," he said, "is up to him. It depends on how strong a will he has."

"Can we see the machine?" I asked.

His face brightened and he beamed at me as he stood up. "Yes," he said, "yes, it's in the next room. I'll show you."

"Jonathan," Kitty said, turning to me with a shocked face. "How can you go forward with it? Didn't you hear him?"

6

I stood up out of the wheel chair on my spindly legs
and wrapped the blanket more tightly around me. If
Kitty hadn't been with me I might have tottered back
out of the room and saved myself. But she was trying
so hard to protect me that she put me into a contrary
mood. She hurried over to help me, but I shook her
off and said I could walk on my own.

Dr. Kack led us out of that false pretense of a sitting area into the real lab, through two intercon-
nected rooms to the back where his machine was set
up.

The room was quite stark, brightly lit, glaring with
white paint and metal equipment. A black counter-
top was littered with bits of wire and tools and a mi-
croscope and a messy stain in the chemical sink that
looked like dried orange juice. I thought I smelled
a bologna and mustard sandwich. He seemed more
comfortable in this space, more at home.

A screen on wheels divided the room into two
parts, a control console on one side and a patient

table on the other. The screen, he told us, blocked harmful radiation. The patient table was steel, scrubbed and shining. Over it, mounted on the ceiling, hung a spaghetti tangle of tubes and wires and glass lenses. The Kwark-King 5.7 did not look as high tech as I had imagined. It looked homemade and I wondered if it was a hoax. He might be experimenting with high levels of electric fields, or flashes of UV light, or something normally quite harmful, and had concocted some preposterous story about quarks to lure terminal patients into his experiments. I hesitated.

"You'll have to take off your clothes," Dr. Kack said.

I let my blanket drop to the floor and began to unbutton my shirt. Kitty stooped and picked up the blanket, clutching it with her thin fingers. She looked frightened, her eyes darting about the room. It didn't occur to me at the time—I was too absorbed in my own drama—but her behavior was not normal. She could have stopped me if she really wanted to. She could have grabbed me about the middle and rushed me out the door in a fury. But she had a passivity about her. She looked angry and scared and outraged and sad all at the same time. Something in her must have been willing to let me go. Maybe even hoping. I was too busy peeling off my shirt and unbuttoning my jeans to pay any attention.

I stood in my underwear, waiting, but Dr. Kack motioned to me. "You need to take those off too," he said. I was embarrassed. The room was so stark and bright that I felt especially naked. Also, I had been wearing the same graying pair of underpants for about a week, and I felt self conscious about how they looked on the inside. I stepped out of them and Kitty hastily took them, as if she had the same embarrassment that I had. She held all of my clothes in a wad. Then I climbed onto the high table and lay down with my feet together and my arms neatly at my sides. The steel tabletop was cold. It hurt my back and shoulders. But the light in the room was so intense, and so focused on the tabletop, that my chest and stomach felt warm and started to prickle with sweat.

Kitty began to cry. I looked up at her. She put her hand over her eyes, crying, her narrow face puckered up. Then she turned to Dr. Kack. "He's so thin," she said. "I didn't know how thin he was under his clothes. Look at how thin he is."

7

"Kitty," Dr. Kack said, gently, a little condescendingly, "you take his clothes behind the screen and sit down. You don't need to watch."

She took my clothes away, but then she came back and stood beside the table, wiping her eyes and nose on the back of her wrist. "I'm okay," she said. "I'll stay right here."

"I'm going to fix you in," Dr. Kack said to me. "It won't hurt yet. I need you to relax."

Now that I was laid out on a table I had become a patient and his tone of voice changed toward me. He spoke clearly and simply in a loud voice.

"He needs to be immobilized," he said to Kitty, then turned back to the table and repeated to me in a raised voice, "I'm going to immobilize you now. It won't hurt yet."

I thought he was going to strap me down at the wrists and ankles. That thought made me nervous. I felt my muscles tense and my body was on the edge of jumping off the table, but I forced myself to lie still and wait. I reminded myself that I could stop the procedure at any time. I had veto power.

He didn't strap me down. The procedure was more complicated and thorough, and finally convinced me that he was telling the truth about his machine, or at least thought he was. He placed a metal mould over me, roughly in the shape of a human body, and bolted it to the tabletop. It arched a few inches above me. A hole in the mould over my face allowed me to breathe, and a second hole on the side allowed my right hand to stick out. I had several inches of room underneath and could still move. I wondered if I was too skinny for the machine and he would have to stop.

"You're doing beautifully," he said looking down through the face hole. "Now I need to put on a breathing mask. He's doing beautifully, Kitty."

He put a rubber contraption to my mouth. "Open," he said, and when I opened my mouth he forced in the device. His hands were not gentle. The device expanded into my mouth and wedged in behind my teeth, pressing down on my tongue. "Very good," he said, but I couldn't object because I couldn't speak. A tube twisted into the back of my mouth, prodding and banging, and found the opening into my windpipe. I choked but could not cough. I was breathing directly into the thin tube that I saw rising up out of the face hole. The tube was clear plastic and I could see a mist forming on the inside of it from my breath.

"You're doing beautifully," he said. He sounded more confident now that I couldn't complain. "The next step is particularly easy. Nothing more than foam, silicon foam."

I could feel the cold foam filling the space under the mould. It surrounded every part of my body. The pressure increased and I thought he had forgotten to turn off the nozzle. My body was being crushed. I could not breathe properly. My muscles hurt and my chest felt squeezed. The air whistled out of the plastic tube in my lungs. When I thought my ribs would crack he turned off the pressure. "Perfect," he said. "Beautifully immobilized. Kitty, he's a beautiful patient. You can move your hand?"

I remembered my right hand. It was jutting out of the contraption and I scrabbled my fingers against the tabletop. "Excellent," he said. "One item left to attend to. Your eyes. Nothing difficult." I saw a tiny clear plastic suction cup like a bathroom plunger loom toward my eye and felt it touch and fix onto the eyeball toward the corner. The suction cup pinched and hurt. Then he suctioned the other eye and I couldn't move my gaze at all. I was fixed staring at the spaghetti tangle of wires on the ceiling.

He used wire spreaders to hold open my eyelids. Then he eye-droppered oil into my eyes to keep them moist and my vision became yellowed and rippled.

I couldn't wink or grin, swallow, shiver, speak, groan, move a toe or a finger, except for my right hand. I could feel my fingernails digging into my palm. I could not breathe. A machine seemed to breathe for me, sending into my lungs a thin trickle of air and then drawing it back out again on its own regular, slow rhythm. I could hear. I could hear quite well. The foam, tight around my ears, seemed to conduct sound. I could hear every click and scrape in the room. I could hear the distinct scuff and snap of Kitty's shoes on the floor. I could hear the gold ring on Dr. Kack's finger clicking against the metal equipment as he handled it. These sounds seemed to transmit through the table and the foam directly into my ears. I could hear their voices, but less clearly.

"Is he comfortable?" Kitty said from far away.

"Yes, of course," Dr. Kack said. "He's doing well."

"Remember to put the alarm in his hand."

"Yes, of course," Dr. Kack said. I saw his hand loom into sight. He was holding a red rubber bulb, the size of a tennis ball, attached to a tube. "Jonathan," he said. "This is the signal bulb. I'm going to put it in your right hand. When you squeeze it, the process will stop. An alarm will sound and the machine will turn off." I felt him pulling open my clenched hand and sliding the bulb in, smooth against my palm. I squeezed it convulsively. "Very good," he said. "Excellent squeeze. Once the procedure begins, you can squeeze it at any time. But I need you to relax now. Kitty," he said, "we're almost ready. Why don't you take a seat behind the protective screen and I'll do a final check."

I could not see Kitty but I could hear the clicking of her shoes across the floor and the gritty squeak of the office chair. Then Dr. Kack walked around the table slowly two times.

"Everything's in place," he said. "Everything's a go. Remember. Hold tight. The longer you can resist the pain, the better the cure. Can you do that? You're already doing beautifully, and your hand is nicely relaxed." My hand was in a fist, crushing the bulb tightly. I felt him grab my fingers, force them open, and take out the bulb. I fumbled with my hand over the tabletop as far as my fingers could reach but the bulb was gone. "You're doing well," he said. "Remember, any time you want to stop, give a squeeze."

Then he stepped away. I heard his footsteps and the squeaky wheels of another chair.

"He's ready?" Kitty said in a muffled voice in the distance. "And we'll know if he's in too much pain?"

"He'll give us a squeeze if he is," Dr. Kack said.

"What's that sound?" Kitty said. "Richard, is that him knocking on the table top?"

"That's the machine warming up," Dr. Kack said. "Funny sound, isn't it? Kitty, don't worry. He'll do beautifully. I think he'll be the one. I think he'll be able to take my machine all the way. I'm very excited. I bet we don't hear that alarm bell at all. That's what I bet. How much do you want to bet?"

"I'm not going to *bet*," Kitty said, in an explosively shrill voice, "on my own *husband*."

8

At first I was in a rage and a panic. That man, that little cheat had trapped me in here with no communication. I would have given his machine an honest try, but he wouldn't even give me the chance. Instead he had to cheat me into it. And now I had no veto power and I would probably die in agony. I was thinking, "This is the end of my life. This, right here. This crazy table."

I could hear my heart knocking and I tried to struggle, but I could not move even a fraction of a millimeter. The pressure of the silicon foam hurt my body. The beating of my heart hurt my chest as if a little steel hammer were hitting my breastbone. The rise in blood pressure must have made my eyes stand out very slightly; at any rate, my eyeballs ached, pressing against the suction cups. I had to stop struggling. I tried to relax and clear my mind, and the pressure lessened slightly. The pain in my chest and eyes sank into a dull ache. I tried not to think about that cheat of a doctor, or about Kitty, or my disease, or death, or anything else. I'm here now, I thought. It is how it is. One way or the other, it will be over in an hour.

Some piece of equipment turned on with a harsh buzzing sound. Then the laser beam hit the bottom of my feet. If I had been holding the bulb I would have squeezed it reflexively, all intentions aside. If I hadn't been held down on the table I would have convulsed like a fish and crashed onto the floor. No person could have withstood that pain for any hope or goal. It vaporized my strength of will. I didn't know about anything except for my feet. The pain lay in a precise plane, like a deli slicer, the rotating blade taking microscopically thin slices one by one, starting from the bottom of my feet and working its way upward. It seemed that every virus particle was a twist of metal, a splinter that needed to be wiggled and wrenched out, torturing the flesh around it. Every bacterium had to be exploded and the shrapnel scraped out with a blunt spatula. Every blemish, every bit of scar tissue, cut with a microscopic scalpel and excised. This was not the torture of a thousand knives. It was six hundred billion knives and drills and lit matches concentrated into one layer of flesh.

By the time the torture reached my ankles I felt the beginning of a separation between my mind and the pain. I could observe the sensation. I felt quite rational and detached. My mind was like a finger poking at my skin, examining the flesh curiously. But although I could feel it, I couldn't see the bug very clearly. I wondered if it was standing right-side-up on top of the glass. It must have run down the side because its jointed knees loomed in front of me larger than coconuts, a formless, shapeless flab of amoeba engulfing my hopes and digesting them.

I had only just stepped in the pond but the leaches had already reached my inner organs. I knew my legs were gone. I bobbed on the surface of the oil. I should have fallen over because there was no counterweight under the floor to hold me upright, but somehow I stood like a plastic outrage and waved at the sunlight. I knew that when the yellow fog rappelled up into the center, when it reached the upper corner, when it touched the green paint it would kill me, so I planted the flag securely to make sure it would remain even after I was dead. I pushed it into the wet cement far enough that even the wind couldn't knock it over. When the metal shaft touched my heart, I was killed, and I felt better. It wasn't so bad being somewhere else and I didn't care about the artificial heat anymore.

I told Kitty it would take a month at least, and she said, Just be patient, and a year goes by more quickly than you think. That's certainly true, I said, because time seems like forever while it's happening but then you measure it with teaspoons and it's all over. It never stays still. I was free enough now to rise like helium above the forest, two hundred feet into the air, and skim over the treetops. The tallest trees actually brushed my face with their shoelaces. I was last seen over Brazil drifting south-southwest. Is that you? I said. Is that you? That is you, Baby, it said. It definitely is. It is so you.

9

"He's just lying there," Kitty said.

I was aware of her voice. I was perfectly aware of her voice and the sight of her face as it drifted across my field of view. I didn't turn my eyes to look. The metal form had been taken off. The foam had been scraped away, although I was aware of a residue all over my body, slightly greasy, as if I were covered in a layer of shaving cream. The suction cups were gone from my eyeballs. The giant spaghetti monster still hung from the ceiling directly above me. I knew where I was. But I didn't move. I wasn't paralyzed: I just didn't want to move. I had come back from a journey that I couldn't quite remember, and I felt absolutely at peace. A Buddha at the zenith of meditation could not have felt as self-contained. The noises and sights around me didn't seem to matter anymore. It's not right to say that I didn't care; that phrase has a harsh connotation. Instead, I didn't *mind* anymore. I felt infinitely indulgent and willing to forgive the world anything, any circumstance it might foist on me, and therefore I saw no point in moving; I simply waited to see what new sensation the world might supply.

"I can feel a pulse," Dr. Kack said. "Is he breathing? Watch closely."

"I think so," Kitty said. "His stomach is going in and out a little."

"JOHN!" Dr. Kack said, cupping his hands to his mouth to project the sound. "There's not even a twitch," he said.

"Nothing," Kitty said.

"He's like all the others," Dr. Kack said.

"He's in a coma," Kitty said.

"Let's pinch his foot," Dr. Kack said.

I could feel him. It was no ordinary pinch. He must have picked up a pair of pliers and tried to rip off a toe. I could hear the clatter of the pliers on the metal tabletop when he put them back down again. "Nothing," he said. "Amazing. Another one."

I thought Kitty might cry, but she didn't. Her face looked stricken. She knew how sensitive my feet had become, and that last demonstration with the pliers must have convinced her. Her hand came trembling up to her lip. "He's dead," she said faintly. "We killed him. Richard, we killed him."

"Well, not strictly speaking," Dr. Kack said. "We gave him the choice. He could have stopped the whole thing any time he wanted, but he let go of the bulb and threw it onto the floor. Maybe he wanted to die?"

Kitty didn't seem to process his words. She stared at me and then turned to Dr. Kack. "We murdered him," she said again.

"Oh, nonsense," Dr. Kack said. "Brace up, Kitty. Besides," he said, coming over and putting his arms around her. "It's a little more convenient for us. Don't you think?"

"Richard," she said, "I never meant for him to—"

"I know," he said soothingly. "Of course you didn't. You tried your best for him. We both did. But let's face it. If he had gotten better, then what? What would we have done? Isn't it better this way? Have you ever read Richard III?"

"Have I *what?*" Kitty said.

"Read Richard III. It's a Shakespeare play."

"I know what it is," Kitty said irritably.

"There's a sensational part where he's just killed her husband and—"

"You're quoting Shakespeare at me?" Kitty said in outrage.

"Well, no, not quoting, not exactly. I just meant. . . ."

10

I listened to them squabble. They sounded more married than Kitty and I ever had. I didn't mind, though, not in my present state. My mind seemed to take possession of the entire situation, to grasp it from all angles at once, and its complexity and symmetry were wonderful. An equilateral love triangle. That, of course, explained her behavior. The missing pieces came into place and I was pleased. Nothing could dent my contentedness, not even the fact of Kitty's betrayal. I was so far from my old self that I could even say to myself, rationally, Jonathan, you betrayed her first. You left her for your disease. She left you for Dr. Kack. Dr. Kack will leave her for his machine. So it all goes around.

Dr. Kack was explaining to Kitty that they had to get rid of my body. "It's okay," he said. "I already thought it through."

"You knew he'd die?" Kitty said. She still looked stricken, and tended to repeat everything he said in a shrill voice.

"No, of course not. But it's always better to be pre-pared. So I took the liberty of stashing away a. . . ," here he rummaged in a cabinet above the sink, "a garment bag."

"We're going to put him in a *garment bag?*"

"Yes, exactly." He unrolled the red plastic garment bag. It had a Pierre Cardin label. "Then we'll put the garment bag into. . . ." I could hear him dragging something heavy across the floor from the corner.

"We're going to put him in a *suitcase?*" Kitty said.

"Yes, exactly. You don't need to sound so skepti-cal. He's quite limp." Here he lifted up my arm and let my hand dangle. "He'll fold."

"And *then?!*" Kitty said, her voice crackling with outrage.

"Then we need to get him out of the building. It's all right. I often bring the suitcase back and forth to my car. I've been carrying it empty for months, so that the guards don't notice anything unusual. You see?" He tapped the side of his head. "I've got a brain after all."

"Then," Kitty said, gripping her frizzy hair and look-ing at him wildly, "your brain has already thought of the problem. The guard saw me drive Jonathan into the building. The receptionist at the entrance saw us walk in together. They all know. Everyone will know. This is crazy. What do we do? What do we *do?*"

"Kitty, calm down," Dr. Kack said, putting his hand

soothingly on her shoulder. "It's nothing we can't handle. Their shifts have changed over. It's a new set now. Obviously you came here with Jonathan, we discussed his options, and then you drove him back home. Then sometime in the very early morning, when you were asleep, he got out of bed and wandered off, poor man, and was never seen again. Must have jumped into the harbor. Obviously depressed. See? There's no reason to worry."

11

They put me into the garment bag and zipped it closed. It smelled like new plastic. It was opaque, but the bright light of the experimental room glowed through the red material and made a fiery aura around me. I felt them lifting me from the table and folding me into the suitcase. It didn't hurt. Nothing could hurt me. They crammed me in, and Dr. Kack had to stand on the top of the suitcase while Kitty closed the latches. I couldn't hear them as well after that. Kitty's voice was more incisive, much more shrill, and I heard her say, "Are you absolutely sure?!" Then I heard Dr. Kack's calmer tones, but the exact words were muffled.

I thought to myself in pure delight, So *this* is what it feels like to be stuffed into a suitcase? I never knew. What a wonderful, new sensation!

Kitty must have gone to the parking lot to drive our car back home. Dr. Kack must have put the suitcase on a dolly. I could feel the smooth sensation of being wheeled down the corridor, and I could hear his long, lanky gait striding calmly behind. I could not hear much else. But I did hear a conversation that occurred in the parking garage. It was between Dr. Kack and the night guard. The dolly stopped, the suitcase was still, and then I heard Dr. Kack talking loudly to someone very far away. I could hear only one side of the conversation. It was pleasant chit-chat and went like this.

"Hiya!"

"Yes."

"Yes!"

"You don't say!"

"Yes. Long day."

"Yes. Going home, finally. You know how it is."

"Yes. You know. Taking a little work home. Never entirely escape, do we?"

"Oh, you know, lab material. Tubes, struts, a lot of chemicals, a few quarks here and there. Nothing too exciting, I'm afraid."

"Yes, sure, I could do with a hand."

Then I could hear the clumping footsteps of the night guard, and the two of them must have lifted the suitcase into the trunk of the car and locked me in.

12

I felt the acceleration of the car and heard the traffic around me, the honking of horns, the grinding
of gears (Dr. Kack didn't have much respect for his
gears), but the sounds were faint. Then for a long
time I was stationary, probably in a driveway or a garage, and the smell of oil and gas seeped into my
garment bag. I think I was in the trunk for about
three days.

I didn't mind. I didn't move a muscle. My eyes
were open and I never blinked. The Kwark-King obviously had given me corneas of steel. They never
dried out. When a normal person is trapped in a
trunk for a few days, he or she probably can't help
thinking about the situation, wondering when the
sicko who put you there will come back, wondering
what will happen to you. But I was past wondering
and feared nothing, and my mind didn't have any
reason to race. I simply was. I sensed. I happily ac-
cepted. I understood each new event as it unfolded.
Why anticipate the next event?

The car started again and I was driven through traffic. Then I was taken out of the car and carried, and I began to sense that I was near water. I was bumped and wheeled, and I could hear seagulls, and I could feel the heat of the sun through the suitcase, and I could smell the salt in the air. I knew I was on a boat. It must have been a small one; it had a choppy motion.

The suitcase was unlatched and the top popped up. Quite suddenly I could hear clearly again. I felt my whole body expanding. Ah, it felt wonderful. Not because I was free. Because it was another sensation. Another bit of experience. Someone pulled me from the suitcase and lay me out on my back on the deck of the boat. Yes, I could tell now that it was a small motor boat and I heard the motor peter out and come to a stop, and then the huge ocean silence came rushing in around me. The air, and the wind, and the slapping of the water on the sides, and everything was so present and so vivid it was wonderful. I was devoutly thankful for the three days in a suitcase, because it was, aesthetically speaking, the perfect preparation for a spin on a boat on the broad Atlantic.

"Why?" said a voice, and it was Kitty's voice, and it was wonderful to hear her voice again! She sounded much calmer than the last time I had heard her. Apparently during the past three days she had gotten over the shock of my demise. Just being rid of me must have improved her mood.

"It might float ashore," said Dr. Kack's voice. They were right next to me. I could hear them nicely. "Anyway, we brought the thing on board, we'd better be seen taking it back off. Although. . . ," he sounded annoyed, "I think the latch on this suitcase is shot."

"Is it bent?" Kitty said.

"It's destroyed," Dr. Kack said. "Maybe I can bend it back in shape at home. Well, I can save the garment bag anyway. Careful, don't rip it."

Kitty began to unzip the garment bag over my face. I saw her as the zipper opened. Her face was concentrated on her work. A glory of sunlight came flooding in and lit up her hair like blonde fire. For a moment, for one moment, she paused and looked at my face and shuddered. Her expression seemed to be all sadness, and horror, and disgust, and relief, put together into one glance. Her face looked so Kitty, so very Kitty, that I almost laughed for pure happiness. I think my lip may have twitched slightly in the direction of a smile because she stopped with her hand on the zipper and looked at me sharply, suspiciously. I didn't move again. She scowled to herself and continued to unzip me. Then she rolled me out of the plastic sack in a very business-like manner and rolled up the garment bag.

"It's okay," she said over her shoulder, while kneeling on the deck and rolling up the bag. "It doesn't smell. I'm sure you can still put a suit in it."

We made a strange tableau. The crowded little deck was a vivid maroon. I lay full length with one foot hanging over the side. I was naked, of course. Kitty sat beside me, her feet down in the driving compartment. She was wearing a black bikini bottom but no top. I suppose there was no reason in the comfortable company of her Doctor paramour. Her torso was so thin I could see her ribs, and her breasts were little triangles pale from a lack of sunlight. She was drinking a diet coke and patting her boney chest with her palm to burp herself. Dr. Kack knelt beside her, fiddling with the suitcase and muttering to himself. I could see what he meant. The top of the case was bent out of shape and wouldn't close right anymore. He was alternately poking at the metal catch and scratching himself in the armpit. He was wearing a pair of yellow swim trunks that were slightly too small for him, and a bit of stomach flapped over the top of the trunks. But otherwise he was skinny. He was hairy all over, except for the top of his head. He should have put on a hat in the sun.

After a while he came carefully along the length of the boat toward me. He had a chain and a padlock, and a heavy iron weight. It was a statue, and I recognized it right away. It came from my living room. It was a two-foot-tall copy of the Venus de Milo, the one without any arms. Venus is supposed to be the god of Love. So I was to be sunk by love.

Dr. Kack wrapped the chain tightly around my right ankle and padlocked Venus to me. Kitty watched him, drinking her coke. She was squinting skeptically, although of course she might have been squinting purely from the bright sun instead of from skepticism.

"Are you sure he'll stay down?" she said. "Won't his foot come off when he decays? I read all about this guy who killed his wife and sunk her in the ocean, and when her feet rotted off she floated back up and they arrested him."

"Not after the Kwark-King," Dr. Kack said, patting my leg proudly. "His foot will never come off."

Then he pushed me over the edge and I plunged down under the sea. I watched the maroon torpedo shape of the boat shrinking above me until it was a speck in the general glitter.

PART II

1

So I sank into the Atlantic ocean, my arms stretched out as if I were crucified and the Venus de Milo towing me down, her own arms, of course, not stretched out, because she didn't have any. The light began to fade. Light does not penetrate very far into the ocean. All around me the world grew dim, full of strange shafts of light and floating motes. The water was already cold at the surface but turned deadly cold as the light faded.

I thought I was sinking more slowly. I couldn't tell if this slowing down was an illusion caused by the dimming of the light, or if it was a real effect of the increasing pressure of water. As that puzzle occupied my mind, something else began to creep into my mind too. For the first time since waking up from the Kwark-King I began to feel afraid.

I didn't worry about drowning. I didn't seem to be killable. I noticed that I was already breathing water. Great plumes of bubbles had come up out of my lungs and now I was gently sucking in and out the seawater itself. I don't think I needed oxygen, but my body was in the habit of breathing and didn't want to stop. I wasn't concerned about the cold, either. My skin registered it, and I didn't mind it. But I didn't like the slow, inevitable fade from everything human, everything terrestrial. I realized suddenly that I was disappearing from the world and sinking into nothingness, and it was a terrible, lonesome, alien feeling.

Because we had motored only a few hours from shore, I didn't think I was sinking into the true depths of the ocean. But it was deep enough to swallow me. Finally, with a soft clunk, Venus hit bottom and I remained hovering over her perfectly still. And then began a very long, very dark phase of my existence.

2

Two times two equals four. Two times four equals eight. Two times eight equals sixteen. This is what you start to tell yourself at the bottom of the ocean to keep a grip on your sanity. Two times sixteen equals thirty-two. Daylight comes, very gray, and then fades, and then comes again, and then fades again. Nothing else changes. My gaze is still upward. My arms are still spread out. I haven't moved. No currents disturb me down here. I am as still as Venus. Two times 65536 is um, okay, 131072.

You might think that, after the first euphoric shock of the Kwark-King, I'd return to a more gritty state of mind and fume and rage against Kitty. True, resentful thoughts did curl through my soul. But with so much blank, gray time to ponder my sins as they say, my thoughts inevitably reached a different place. Never mind Kitty's failings. I had known about them or suspected them for a long time. What about my own failings?

Why was I so terrible to Kitty? Why was I a self-centered dick? Normally I don't like these terms of obscenity. It's too easy to condemn a human being by comparing him or her to a piece of reproductive anatomy. But sometimes it is just the right word. Dick, dork, putz, prick. The right word for me is Dick.

I got sick from a fling. I had the fling when Kitty went away for a week to a conference of professional art critics. She wrote a regular art column for a newspaper. In the room the women come and go, talking of Michelangelo. And two times 2097152 is 4194304. I am getting good at my powers of two.

On the other hand, she had a fling too, and she and her fling killed me. Somewhat unintentionally. Let's be honest. He would have been thrilled if I had proven his machine. If I had stood up at the end, shook his hand, congratulated him, thanked him, put on my clothes, and walked out the door with Kitty? He would have been pumping his fists in triumph. He had it rigged either way. If I died, he got Kitty. If I survived, then his machine was a success. I'm guessing Kitty was the consolation prize and he would have rather had the other one. But I admit, I am biased against him; I'm inclined to think of him as a Prick.

But Kitty? I won't break out the slang for the female genitalia, because I can't feel any resentment toward her. I am positively happy that she is so faulty a person, because it gives me something to work with, something to become reconciled to. Yes, sure, so she helped put me in a suitcase and watched me get dumped in the ocean. But you have to consider the essential jaggedness of the human soul. It has its ups and downs. And that jaggedness is exactly what makes it so beautiful. If a rugged, splintery mountain were bulldozed and spread around and generally smoothed into a gravel parking lot, it wouldn't be a beautiful mountain anymore. Kitty is beautiful and jagged. She is herself, her essential Kittyness, and I am not to question it. I notice that my right hand is tingling. I wonder if the Kwark-King is wearing off?

I will set myself the eternal task of un-Dicking myself. The key is to concentrate on Kitty. To float in purgatory, away from all people and all pleasures, anchored by the foot in the dark and the gray. I can never annoy her again, which is an improvement. She can live her life up above, however she chooses, and I can stay down here and keep her in my heart and wonder about my right hand.

3

I don't know how many years passed. It might have been as long as twenty. Frankly, it might have been only half a year. Time has a way of stretching out under the circumstances. One day, at around noon when the gray light was at its brightest, when I was in the middle of thinking about Kitty, trying to imagine her face like a giant balloon floating above me anchored by a long rope to my heart, and imagining, as vividly as I could, the feeling of the rope tugging on my aorta, the pain of love you see, in the middle of this very typical occupation of mine, something new happened. An object drifted across my line of vision and I . . . I blinked.

I did. I made my first voluntary movement since waking up from the Kwark-King. I blinked. And I looked again. In the gray light, I saw a mouse. It was a little black mouse with bulbous black eyes. It was swimming. Its tiny paws were treading and its tail was streaming out behind. It swam like a most bizarre spermatozoan directly over me, only about a yard from my face, and passed me and disappeared. What, I thought, is a mouse doing down here? That mouse should be dead.

After about a minute, something else swam into view. It was a cat. The cat was a large gray tabby. At least, it looked gray in the dim light. It was treading also, its mouth slightly open and its teeth gleaming, its eyes narrowed to slits as it pursued the mouse. It swam past and disappeared.

Then I was alone again.

At first I thought I had finally cracked. I was hallucinating. In trying to envision Kitty as clearly as possible I had generated a cat. And a mouse. I wasn't sure how the mouse got into it. Poor, poor me.

The correct explanation, however, did not take me long to realize. I had just seen two fellow experimental subjects of Dr. Kack's. This place in the Atlantic must have been his usual dumping ground. He must have motored out here with a suitcase full of comatose animals and emptied the whole thing over the side. Down they went, twirling and twining in the water. Thump onto the bottom of the ocean. These two specimens must have been dumped off before me. They had had time to wake up and move again. Their state of passive euphoria was wearing off, and they were coming into the possession of their own bodies.

If that mouse and that cat can move around, I

thought, why can't I?

So I turned my head. I looked to my left, and I looked to my right, and then I looked down toward my feet. A normal person would have had a stiff neck after all that time. A normal person, actually, would have been dead. But my neck was in perfect order. My vertebral links functioned smoothly. I felt great. And when I looked down I saw, all at once, why it was that Venus de Milo had touched down on the ocean floor with a clunk. When you think of it, the ocean floor should be covered with a layer of squishy mud. But I wasn't on the ocean floor; I was on the iron deck of a ship. All this time, years possibly, I had been anchored to a shipwreck and hadn't even known it because my head was tilted back and I was looking up.

4

I was near the bow of the ship. Behind me a great rusty rectangle of metal rose up and disappeared in the darkness, one of the superstructures on the deck. The railings around me dripped with icicles of rust and growth. The floor was pitted. I could see rivets in a neat line, connecting two large plates of metal. A massive cylinder of metal stuck out over the side of the deck, a heavy gun.

I was floating about three yards above the deck, anchored to it by the chain attached to my foot. I bent over, grasped the chain, and began to pull myself down. The chain was already rusty and covered in growth, and a fine dust rose up from it and spread out through the water as I touched it. When I reached the bottom, I saw my Venus standing upright like a figurehead, peering out through the railings at a great blackness of water. The light was so dim that I could not see the ocean floor over the side of the boat.

The iron wall near me was full of empty windows.

They were round, small windows that only a skinny person could have climbed through. Kitty, I thought, is it okay if I climb in there and rummage around? I want to find a workroom, a room with some tools in it, to cut this chain. Is that okay? Do you mind? I didn't get an answer, of course. So I picked up Venus in my arms and walked toward the windowed wall. At every footstep on the deck I created a little explosion of silt.

I wormed into the window. The edges were jagged. There was no glass left, but the metal rim was broken and sharp. I didn't mind. I had puncture-resistant skin. I noticed, as I was grasping the sides of the window, that my right hand was puffy, like a hand left in the bath too long. It didn't hurt, though, and I could move my fingers okay.

I thought I would be in blackness inside, but instead I found that the roof was gone. I was in the same dim gray light. I was in a narrow corridor that stretched out in front of me with dark open doorways to either side. I couldn't see the end of the corridor; it was too far away in the dimness.

I was eager to explore. I had spent years, possibly, thinking that I was cut off from all things human, in a solitude as complete as outer space. And yet here was a human house, and I had been on its front porch the entire time. Human window holes, to let in light. Human railings, for human hands to lean on. A human cannon, to kill other humans with. It was all so comforting. I felt close again to the world above.

I went into the nearest open door, moving slowly through the density of water. The room was black, except for the rectangle of dim light that fell in through the doorway, but I felt my way around it very carefully. It was a tiny room. It might have been an office. It had a metal counter, a metal chair, a set of metal shelves screwed to the walls, and a femur on the floor. I didn't know it was a femur until I took it back outside into the light. When I realized what it was, I put it back into the room where I found it.

I explored every room I came to, moving systematically down the corridor. The rooms were all small. I think rooms are that way on a ship to optimize space.

The ship must have been too far down for life. I didn't see any fish, or shrimp, or octopuses, or anything else that I normally associated with oceans. I did see the mouse. It swam out of a stateroom and streamed away. I suppose the cat was lurking around somewhere. Of course, if the cat ever caught the mouse, it wouldn't be able to kill it. The mouse would have been tooth-impervious.

I found the kitchen. It was larger than the other rooms and full of rusty metal rims, which I think were the remains of pots and pans. I found a lot of handles of knives. I don't know why the handles survived but the blades didn't. I also found a saw blade that might have been used to cut up large frozen pieces of beef. I took the saw outside to the corridor, sat cross-legged on the floor, and right there I sawed at the chain on my ankle. A lot of the teeth were worn out and rusty. After fifteen minutes the remaining teeth broke off, and the saw was no good at all. The chain had only a small scratch on it.

I wasn't upset. I had years ahead of me to search the ship and look for saws. I thought I'd get that chain off eventually, and in the mean time it didn't hinder me except that I had to carry Venus with me everywhere I went.

Venus, I thought, Venus, we are going to live here together. I am going to explore the lower levels and the upper levels and make a home. And I will have a pet cat and a pet mouse. And maybe even find some books, although I'll have some trouble reading them in this light. I hope they're picture books. And I will be okay for a long time.

Jonathan, Venus said to me (I mean, I imagined her saying to me), that sounds great, but what about Kitty? Are you going to forget about Kitty? How can you live close to other people again, take up residence in a ship and get domestic with a mouse and cat, when you're supposed to be in limbo meditating on Kitty?

Jeez, you're right, Venus, I thought. I'm losing my concentration. I should have stayed perfectly still and minded my own business. That darn mouse distracted me!

Listen, Venus said. It isn't the mouse. It's the ship. It's too close to the outer world. Go deeper, go further. You better go away and live by yourself again. You need to keep your mind on what's important.

Venus, I thought, you're right.

I carried her back outside and placed her on the deck facing the bow. She was too short to look over the top of the railing, but she could look out between the first and second cables. The bow of the boat faced east. I knew this because in the mornings the light slanted down very slightly from that direction, and in the evenings, the light lingered in the opposite direction. I remembered reading once that, to the east, somewhere about halfway across the ocean, was a ridge. A kind of mountain range under the water. And that ridge at the center of the ocean seemed like an appropriate, lonely place I could go, where I wouldn't be distracted and I could meditate on Kitty.

Venus, I thought, tomorrow morning, as soon as it's light out, I am going to climb over the railing and walk east. I am going to walk across the floors of silent seas right to the mid-ocean ridge. And I am going to take you with me. What do you think about that?

5

Scientifically speaking, here is what happens to a normal human body at the bottom of the ocean. The air is squeezed out of its lungs. The water in the body is compressed to the same density as the surrounding water. The body actually gets smaller. This squeezing of the body is very slight, almost undetectable, because water resists compressing. The density of water is only very slightly greater at the bottom of the ocean, despite the enormous increase in pressure. The body becomes neutrally buoyant, meaning it is effectively weightless. The person dies.

Here is what happens to a human body that has been Kwark-Kinged and sent to the bottom of the ocean. The air is squeezed out of the lungs. The water in the body, and all other bodily materials, are incompressible and indestructible. The body, therefore, is not able to equilibrate with the surrounding water pressure. The body is less dense, by a very tiny amount, and tends to float. If the body has a large iron sculpture tucked under its arm, then the body can walk along the ocean floor in an awkward manner. If the iron sculpture is dropped, it will go straight down and the body will go slowly up, never the two to meet again, unless the body can get to the surface and find another weight to send it back down again. Happily, I had a chain connecting me to Venus. Therefore, every time I accidentally dropped her I would float up a few yards, come to a stop, and then haul myself down again, hand over hand.

One central point of these physical considerations is that it was *not possible* for me to rise above the ocean floor. I was anchored to it and had no other option except to walk.

So I walked.

I walked across flat plains with a hard ground under an inch of dust, churning up a wake of blackness behind me. I walked up hills with stony tops. I walked down into depressions filled with a mud like thin oatmeal, five hundred feet over my head. I couldn't walk on top of that stuff, so I had to walk through it, hoping I didn't get too far off direction and end up in circles.

Most of the time I was in darkness. Light can penetrate only so far. Maybe a giant squid eye could have seen its way around, but my human eye, even though it was Kwark-Kinged and had a perfect correction and perfect clarity, the keenest sight of any human on earth, still could see nothing but blackness and imagination below 500 yards. And I was often five to ten times below that.

I developed a blind man's sensitivity of touch.

I developed an uncanny sense of hearing.

Try the following experiment. Blindfold yourself. Better yet, pick a friend and blindfold him. Then turn him around to induce spatial confusion. Then ask him to walk in a straight line toward a wall. He will probably stop just before whacking into the wall. "I don't know," he'll say, "I feel like there's something in front of me. It must be ESP."

Now try the same experiment but plug his ears. This time, he'll disjoint his nose before coming to a stop. "Ouch!" he'll say. "Why did you let me do that? I thought we were friends!"

The fact is, with his ears unplugged, your friend will hear a change in sound resonance as he approaches the wall. He will sense that he is approaching a confined space.

This is human echolocation. It is an amazing ability that we rarely use. We are not very good at it compared to dolphins, or whales, or bats. Bats are astounding. Do you know the expression, "You couldn't hit a barn door at one yard"? That is what bats say about us, and it is true. Bats can hit a moving bug in the dark.

All the same, it is amazing how much echolocation a human can develop out of necessity. I came to have an uncanny sense of the space around me. I knew if there was a boulder in front of me, or to one side or the other. I knew if I was approaching a hill or a sudden drop. I knew these things in the dark, in the absolute dark, because the links of my chain grated against each other at every step; I rattled them like rosary beads; and the sound came back to me with a peculiar resonance. I got used to judging that resonance.

But no amount of echolocation could get the points of my compass straight. To be certain that I was walking east, I had to rely on the hills. Sometimes I walked up a hill tall enough to bring me into the light, and then I'd watch the gradual slanting of the long, shimmering beams from east to west as the day progressed.

Life, both vegetable and animal, inhabited those shallow spots. Ordinarily, when you climb a very tall mountain, you reach a tree line above which plants and animals don't consistently survive. Here, under the ocean, the pattern was reversed. If I walked up a hill, I would cross a life-line above which the world was suddenly populous. Even though I was on my way to solitude and a mountain hermitage, I had a lively journey.

I met a school of tuna. I think they were tuna. I am more used to the tuna that you find in a can, so it is possible that I got the wrong species. But some type of large fish in a great school flashed around me. I could reach out a hand and touch them, and they weren't shy. I thought they were curious, staring at me out of sideways eyes.

I met a long line of lobsters. Thousands of them marched in single file, end to end, across the ocean floor. I don't know why.

I met a milky fog of billions, trillions of tiny animals, wriggling, twitching, shooting in random directions.

I met a pod of dolphins at the top of a particularly tall hill. There were six dolphins, and two of them came close to me and stared at me. One of them bumped me on the chest with its bottle snout.

"How do you do?" I said. I couldn't speak underwater, especially without any air in my lungs, but I mouthed the words.

The dolphin replied, "!!!!!!glglglglglglg."

"Do you know how far it is to the mid-oceanic ridge?"

"!!!!!!!"

"I see. And do you know if I am going in the right direction?"

The dolphin shook its head, then nodded its head, then bumped me in the chest again.

"Could you be less, um, ambiguous?" I said, but the dolphin swam away.

I met a whale. It was dead. It was a great whale-shaped blob on the ocean floor, covered with slugs and starfish, an oasis.

I met a shark. I met a lot of sharks, actually. They are fast and graceful and beautiful. But it is very difficult for a shark to catch a fish. The prey and the predators are pretty well matched.

I was attacked once. A huge shark, a great gray missile of a shark three times my own length, with unblinking eyes and a cut down the side of its pointed snout, circled me as I was walking along the top of a stony plateau. Maybe it had gotten into a fight with another shark. Or maybe it had tangled with a fishing hook. The cut on its face was slowly spreading open, exposing a yellowish, infected flesh inside and a white piece of its cartilaginous skeleton. I felt sorry for it. But I did not encourage it. I kept walking and did not look too closely in its eye.

Finally it turned over and snatched at me with its teeth. I don't know how sensitive a shark's teeth and gums might be, but I was tooth-impervious and the shark must have felt like you do when you bite down on a little bit of walnut shell embedded in the apple and walnut pie that you expected to be a soft mush. It dropped me and swam away.

This attack didn't frighten me. For a moment, in the shark's jaws, I was aware of its power. I was a rag in its mouth. But I was an unkillable rag. Venus, on the other hand, was only a defenseless piece of metal. She came through the ordeal with a three-inch scratch on her patina of rust. After the attack I decided to wrap the chain around my body and neck, and sling Venus like a pendant on my chest, so that in future attacks I could throw my arms around her and protect her.

A few minutes after the attack I noticed that my right hand hurt. It had gotten pinched in the shark's jaws. I must not have noticed at the time in the excitement of being snatched up, but now it felt like somebody had hit it with a post maul.

For months my right hand had been getting bigger. I couldn't ignore it. It was noticeably larger than the other one. The fingers were turning into sausages, the palm into a sponge. Now I inspected it and saw a strafe of tooth impressions across the palm.

My right hand, of course, sticking out the side of the Kwark-King, had never gotten the full blast of the laser. It had held up better than a normal hand, but it had its limits. It was becoming water logged and slowly disintegrating. Someday it would turn into a great shapeless jelly and fall off. It was an open question whether the rest of me might go the same way, eventually.

6

Don't be fooled by all the life I saw on my journey. Most of the time I was alone. The abiding truth of the ocean is that it is dark and it is empty.

7

But it is beautiful. I wish you could have seen it, Kitty.

8

There is no place on earth better suited to meditation than the mid-ocean ridge. It is really a great long line of volcanoes. I explored them up and down, north and south, climbing over their slopes and ridges and looking into caves, before finding exactly the spot for me. I found a ledge high up on a mountainside, perhaps a thousand feet above the ocean floor. The ledge was ten feet wide and perfectly smooth, almost like glass. It had a single round stone in the center welded to the floor volcanically. This stone was just the size and shape for a sitting stool. Beside the sitting stool, a great orange crack opened on the rising surface of the mountain, a vent into a volcanic interior. That vent lit up the ledge and flickered on the glass-like floor.

I sat on the stool with Venus in my lap, my bare feet on the hot glass floor, and gazed into the vent. I didn't bother to blink. Dark plumes of minerals, dissolved in the superheated water, floated up. These smokes and steams flickered and glowed from beneath.

There is something inexplicable about fire that frees the imagination. If you give the brain nothing, only darkness, it might run thin on ideas, but when you give it that flamelight that never stays still, the brain is mesmerized, the imagination is inspired, shapes and people and words and events unfurl. Just so on a much grander scale with a volcanic vent, when you are right up against it.

9

Kitty times Kitty equals Kitty. Kitty, you wouldn't believe what I've done for you. I've walked and walked till my Kwark-Kinged legs were tired out. I've climbed over mountains. I've given up my right hand to you. Look at it. It's getting worse every year. It's so puffy you can't even see the shark bite anymore. It'll fall off any time now. But it was worth it, because look at all the things I've seen. I'll show you in my imagination. I'll scroll through it for you. Slide one. Look at this whale. I tell you, have you ever seen anything like it? This huge rotting pile crawling with life? It's amazing. Look at the size of that slug. You never were really big on slugs. But you were an art critic, so imagine this thing as art, hung up on the wall in the MOMA. The whole ocean, for that matter. It's all art. See what I mean? See?

10

But is that the right way? Venus said. Admire her, sure. Think about her, sure. But talk to her? That seems disrespectful. Talking to her when she's not around is like making yourself a Kitty doll and playing with it. That's like—

Venus, put a sock in it. What do you know about love anyway?

Ho ho, Venus said, that's ironic. I'm a Greek goddess. I know everything.

Actually you're a Roman goddess. I guess your omniscience didn't quite extend to that fact. Hm? Ha ha. Take that.

Oh give me a break, Venus said. Ancient Romans, ancient Greeks, they're all the same. The point is, your meditation has become, well, self-centered. It's all about you, what you've seen, what you're feeling.

Sure it is, I said. But Venus, Kitty is me. Kitty is my soul, my heart, my beginning and my end, whenever that will be. Hence thinking about me is the same thing as thinking about her. If it weren't for Kitty I'd have walked west instead of east, and gotten back to the continental US. I'd be working the stock room in CVS, or something. But instead here I am as far from humanity as I can get, sitting naked on a hot rock, meditating.

Very romantic, Venus said.

It is, I said. Jeez, don't be so sarcastic all the time.

Do you even remember who she is? Venus said.

Vividly.

Do you remember what she looks like?

Vividly.

Do you remember the two cords that stand out on the back of her neck? Do you remember her frizzy hair? And her shocked expression? And her spike heals that made her a little bit tippy?

Vividly.

And you can still love that?

Venus, I believe you're jealous.

Up yours, Venus said. Don't insult me. I want you to love, but you sit here loving yourself. I want you to love what's best and noblest in Kitty, but between the two of us we can't think what that is. Now tell me, what's going on?

Oh Venus, Venus. Are you going Socratic on me? Are you trying to get me to explain what Love is?

That'd be a trick, Venus said. Nobody's explained it yet.

11

I don't know if it was day or night, or what year or what time of the year, but suddenly the space around me began to glow with a white light. There are many possible causes of a white glow. One is visitation by a particularly luminescent deity. Another is an anomalous surge in heat that is so extreme it causes stones to glow white-hot. Neither of these explanations turned out to be correct, however. The white glow flickered, shifted, jiggled, and I realized that it was casting a shadow of my head on the rocky wall in front of me. The light must therefore come from behind me.

I stood up and turned around. Hovering in the water a few yards away was a yellow flying saucer. It was metallic and had mechanical arms with claw-like grippers, a pair of bright headlights, and several round portholes. In the forward porthole I saw, distorted from the immense thickness of the glass, a human face peering out at me. So I smiled and waved. I had to wave with my left hand because my right hand was pretty much shot by then. It looked more like a slug than a hand.

I suppose the man in the submersible was not expecting a naked human with a slug for a right hand and Venus de Milo hanging on its chest by a rusty chain.

The man's face expressed the most profound fear I have ever seen on the human map. I couldn't hear him, but his mouth opened wide in an unmistakable scream with concentric wrinkles etched around his lips rippling back to his ears. His hair shot out all over his head like a trick wig. Boing! The submersible backed away and fled into the darkness of the ocean.

I never learned who he was, or what his scientific mission might have been. I don't know if our chance encounter changed his life, or made him quit science, or made him go insane or convert to Satanism. I never met him again. His role in my life was profound for these simple reasons:

He roused me from my meditations.

He proved that I was still within the reach of the human world and therefore not yet free of all distraction.

I stood and looked around at the blackness of the ocean, and the red volcanic glow, and the reflection in the glassy floor under my feet, and I said, Venus, I think maybe the time has come for the last step of the journey. I think I am going down the vent. If I can't meditate on unconditional love immersed in a lava pit, then I can't do it anywhere.

Hold tight to me, Venus said. We've been together a long time; don't lose me now.

12

I crawled into the shaft, fell a long way, bumped against an inner ledge, then sank further. I got turned around and drifted down head first, then got turned back and went feet first. Every time I got stuck, I wriggled out of the trap and went deeper. Once I reached a bend in the shaft and had to wriggle sideways for a few yards before I found another straight drop. I couldn't see very well. My eyes were open, but everything around me was minerals and flickering lights. The minerals formed a film over my skin and corneas. After a while I reached actual magma and sank into it. The glutinous stuff closed over my eyes and glowed bright orange into my pupils. It was like putting my eye directly against a light bulb. It was the most intense light I had ever experienced, especially after decades of shadow under the ocean.

My hand was long past any pain. Most of the nerves were shot anyway, but I had just enough feeling left to know that it was burnt to a crisp in the first thirty seconds. The rest of me seemed as impervious as ever.

I hugged both my arms to my chest around Venus.

Here are a few important facts that I did not know at the time, but have learned since. Magma, or molten rock, can be a range of different temperatures. Hot magma is runny whereas cool magma tends to be thick, something like oatmeal, a material that also thickens as it cools. At most, magma is about 1200 degrees Celsius. Usually it's cooler than that. Iron, however, melts at 1535 degrees Celsius. Venus, therefore, was safe.

I could feel her heating up against me, but soon realized that she was not melting. She was a little soft, and when I felt over her face I thought her features were getting blurred. But she was still her essential self.

The chain, by the way, was made of steel. Steel is iron with certain metallic impurities mixed into it. The impurities make it stronger, but also lower its melting temperature. I don't know the exact alloy of steel used to make this particular chain, but it became soft like wet clay and slowly dripped off of me.

I was free.

Venus and I were bound together only by my arms tightly wrapped around her, one arm with a hand, the other with a stump. And in that state we floated in nothingness, with no up, no down, and no time.

Part III

1

There is a kind of treatment that you can get if you think you are crazy or out of balance or generally exhausted with life. The treatment is called Birthing. It can be done in a variety of different ways. Some psychoanalysts will push you into a swimming pool with your hands tied behind your back, and then jump in and pull you back out. That feeling of amniotic helplessness followed by the dramatic rescue is intended to make you feel better about life. Give you a new beginning, so to speak.

Another type of Birthing is to roll you up in a rug and beat the rug with a stick. This treatment is supposed to mimic birth contractions in a vagina, and you are expected to struggle and fight your way out. The intention here is to give you a feeling of empowerment.

Every so often, somebody undergoing a Birthing treatment drowns or gets beaten to death.

I experienced the ultimate Birthing. I crawled into Mother Nature's womb and she gave one mighty birth contraction and popped out the pup, sending me spinning into the world of human civilization.

2

Many people have been at the center of a volcanic eruption, but most or all of them died in the process. I may possibly be the only one to survive and bear witness. The experience is not as exciting to describe as one might expect, because I felt and heard only a little of it and saw none of it. Motion, noise. More motion, more noise. I could tell I was moving very, very fast, and I kept my arms tight around Venus. Sound travels best through thick materials, hence you hear better underwater and even better immersed in lava. The roar ranged from the lowest notes that shake whole mountains to the highest piercing whistles like a thousand bats. The roar began to fade and the shrieks and whistles increased as the magma reached seawater. The temperature dropped sharply. From a limp doll tossed around by the eruptive force, within half a second I became a statue encased in rock. I was in blackness. I could feel my statue self rolling and tumbling in the water for weeks. Volcanic gasses may have been trapped in the stone casing around me, or it may be that the disturbed ocean currents kept me moving. In any case, I wasn't obviously sinking back to the ocean floor. I was drifting, sometimes feet up, sometimes head up, sometimes clunking against other objects. I wondered if I was bumping against reefs, or sharks, or shipwrecks, or shores.

3

I heard a voice perfectly clearly just beside me. "Yo, Kenny."

"What?" The second voice came from farther away.

I could feel the water slowly seeping out of the rock around me. Wherever I was, I was moving up and down, side to side, in a corkscrew motion. The sarcophagus of stone was so tight around me that I couldn't move. My eyes were open but I saw only the blackness of the inside of stone. Maybe I saw a hint of gray. I could feel heat coming through the stone and guessed that I was lying in sunlight in the open air.

"Take a look."

"At what?"

"At this."

"Don't pull another four-headed fish on me, Don. It isn't funny."

Don laughed noisily. "It's not a four-headed fish. Take a look."

"Some piece of shit garbage."

"No, wait, let me get it out of the net."

I was rolled and bumped and lay face up.

"Jeeeezus Christ," Don said. "Will you look at that."

"You think it's a body?" Kenny said in a hushed voice, so close to me that I could tell he was crouching. I felt him push at me. "How come it's all petrified?"

"It's giving me the willies," Don said. "Don't, don't touch it anymore, Kenny. It might be a mummy. You know how mummies have curses and things."

"It's a statue," Kenny said. "Anyway, who ever heard of an ocean mummy?"

"It could happen."

"No it couldn't," Kenny said.

"Yes it could," Don said.

"No, it couldn't. What are you, stupid? Mummies come from the desert."

"So? What if somebody dug up a herd of mummies, shipped 'em cargo crate, and the ship sank. Bang, here's our mummy floating around."

"Well. . . ," Kenny sounded thoughtful. "I suppose it could be." I felt something tap sharply on the rock over my face. "But it's too hard. Mummies are all leathery. I think it's a statue. Like you said, it probably came off a shipwreck."

"What's it a statue of?"

"A Greek god or something. I bet it's worth money," Kenny said, meditatively.

"What's it, the god of ugliness?" Don said. "That is one ass-ugly god."

"Yeah," Kenny said, tapping again on the outside of the stone just over my nose, "but it's covered over in crud it's been in the ocean so long. Under all that crud it's probably a naked woman with no arms. Know what I mean?"

"Maybe it's gold," Don said. "Let's scrape off the crud and see if it's gold."

"It wouldn't be *gold*," Kenny said, in a disgusted tone, "or it wouldn't *float*. It'd be at the bottom of the ocean."

"It could too be gold," Don said.

"No, it couldn't."

"It could be hollow."

"Well," Kenny said, "I suppose you're right. But I bet it's worth more if we sell it to a museum. We better not scrape at it, or we'll drop the price."

"I know a guy who owns a kind of art shop," Don said. "We can ask him. He bought some driftwood off me once."

4

I was propped up in the corner of the shop. I was there for months and could tell the size and layout of the little shop by sound. We were on the ground floor and I could hear the traffic outside. I could see gray during the day through a fine web of cracks forming over my face, and, at night, the dim red and blue of street signs gleaming in the window. Every morning I heard the shop owner pulling back the metal grating over the door and setting up for the day.

Sometimes customers stood in front of me and touched me. If they loomed in close to peer at me, I'd hear their breathing especially loudly.

"Yep," the shop owner would say, coming over to the corner. "Statue Holding a Statue. See how the big one is holding the little one in its arms? It's Greek, you know. Thucydides' last sculpture. He roughed it out in black granite, but before he could smooth it over and put in the features, a chip of it flew into his brain and killed him. Pliny writes about it. Very fascinating story. A friend of a friend inherited it from the Rockefeller-Ryes art collection. I was lucky to get possession of it in a trade. It's yours for twenty thousand."

After a while the price came down to ten thousand. Then five thousand. There I remained. Considering that he had bought me for a hundred dollars, I thought he was being overly ambitious. Thucydides notwithstanding, I was apparently one ugly sculpture and didn't fit anyone's decor.

Finally a more knowledgeable customer inspected me carefully. When the shop owner told him about Thucydides, the man laughed so hard that I could smell his breath through the micro cracks in the stone. He must have eaten a Reuben sandwich followed by some chocolate mint.

"Save it for someone else," he said. "This is water-carved volcanic basalt. It's a natural formation. I love it. You know what I like about it? Look at the eyes. You can almost see a gleam back there under the cracks, as if there's a spirit trapped in it. It's fantastic. I'll give you two-hundred-fifty for it."

"*Two-fifty?* Do you *know* how hard it was to wedge this thing out of the cave, carry it a mile on my back, hoist it into my truck and schlep it across country? This thing is from Colorado and the gas itself was more than two-fifty. Plus the chiropractor for my back. I'm not selling it for less than a thousand."

"All right, keep your hat on. I'll buy it for five hundred. Any more and I might as well go carve my own."

5

"Once again," the museum guide said, "we are looking at found art. It's a beautiful example." Her voice resonated in the hall. The space rustled with whispers and the tapping of shoes on a marble floor. "He calls it Demon in Disguise. Of course, Camptiffler is a master of found art. He has an exquisite eye for the accidental form. He found this piece in Hawaii. Notice the eyes. It has quartz deposits deep inside, and when the light is right you can see a glitter through the cracks on the surface. Like a demon peering out at you. It's one of the most expensive pieces in his collection, and I think you can see why."

6

"Mom, this is so fucking boring, can't we go home?"

"*Michael!* You watch your language in public!"

"Yeah, yeah, whatever, look, it's a room full of rocks. Rocks on pedestals. Funny looking rocks. Whoop-de-fucking-do. If I had a sledgehammer, it'd be a lot more exciting. Tommy has a. . . ." (The voice trails away in the background noise.)

7

The janitor's broom sounds like an animal breathing in sharp gasps. It grows louder and then pauses in front of me. "Hello Demon. Another long day? Yeah. I know how it is. You and me both. Hm?"

I'm a favorite of his.

Silence and dimness during the night.

Then the jingle of the morning guard stumping through and opening the exhibits. The morning guard never says a word to me or any of the other statues. I don't even know if it is a he or she.

Then the crowds. I can sense hundreds of people together in the blended echoes of their voices. Thousands in a day.

It is very distracting. This is not the inner peace of the ocean.

Venus, Venus, how did it come to this? What should we do?

Hush, says Venus.

She doesn't talk to me much anymore. The place is too distracting. Too many voices, too much commotion for the slow deep decades of meditation. But I choose to stay where I am. There are two very good reasons.

First, I can't move anyway. I suppose if I tried very hard I might break out a hand or a foot. Sometimes I wonder how the museum guide would react if the Demon Within was suddenly no longer entirely within.

The second reason is that, sometimes, once every three or four days, rising up over the whispers and rustlings, I hear a scrap of sound that is almost like Kitty's voice. My whole body tingles and I listen as hard as I can, but the voice sinks back into the general murmur. Kitty, Kitty, are you really out there? Are you still alive? Do you remember me? I know it's probably not her, but every time, I feel a rush like a drug and my heart beats hard against the inside of my stone shell.

8

It was almost closing time and the crowds had thinned. It was a rainy day. I could always tell the weather by the smell of the people. The rain and mud and ozone were unmistakable even in the climate-controlled space of the museum, and the bad weather must have kept the crowds down all day. The room was silent for minutes at a time.

"It's quite nice," a man said in front of me in a hushed voice. Because the room was missing its usual background murmur, I could hear him clearly. "It really is compelling. It's a trick of the brain, you know. We look at a twisty piece of rock and the social part of the brain goes into overdrive and figures out how to make a human body out of it. Man-in-the-moon syndrome, you know."

"Yes, yes," a woman's voice said quietly beside him. "You make a science lecture out of everything." She had the slightly wobbly voice of an older woman. My skin and spine felt like a bed of needles, and for an instant I didn't know why. Those parts of my body had recognized her voice half a second before I did. But then I realized that it was Kitty. I was certain. It was not just the addictive drug of a hauntingly similar voice. It was her actual voice layered over with age.

"The only real question," she said, "is whether you like it or not. You don't need to play the scientist."

"I told you, I like it. It's very nice. And you?"

She was silent for a long time, staring at me. I thought I could feel her shadow. There must have been a small spotlight on me heating up the stone, because when visitors came especially close to look at me I could feel the coolness of a shadow. Now I felt her shadow on my body. She must have been holding her breath.

Then she stepped back. "Oh," she said faintly. "It's so. . . ."

I never found out what she meant to say. Somehow, trembling, heart beating hard, I must have shifted a critical amount in my stone sarcophagus and I toppled forward. She shrieked and jumped back. I smashed onto the hard floor and lay face down.

A guard came running over and I heard a lot of angry voices.

"That's a five million dollar sculpture!" the guard shouted.

The man shouted back, "It could have killed her! We aught to sue!" Now I placed his voice. It was older, thinner, shriller, but it was Dr. Kack's. I tried to sit up, but I was still too much of a statue to move. Also I was afraid. I was afraid of meeting her face to face. I had never meant to see her again. I had promised myself that I would never ruin her life again.

Kitty and Dr. Kack were whisked out of the room. A babble of voices surrounded me. A paramedic team specialized for the injured sculpture put me in a stretcher and hustled me to a workroom. I knew it was a workroom because of the smell of rubbing alcohol and glue and paint and fresh wood. There I was inspected.

The master restorer said, "It's pretty well cracked. You got your structural fracture here, and it spirals around the back there. This won't stay together. We could glue it with epoxy, but you'd see the seam. We could drill a hole up through the middle of it and put in a rod. That would steady it. But you'll never get rid of that crack. You tell me, I'll do what you want. I'm just saying, you'll never get rid of the crack."

I was in that room for several days. The stone over my face was more cracked than before and I could see, dimly, the outline of a brass light fixture in the ceiling. Sometimes I saw faces hovering over me, staring down, always frowning, always very grave. Some of these faces were attached to ties and suits, and I figured they were the rich contributors. Others were attached to old flannel shirts and I decided they must be the restorers. Once somebody stuck a finger through a crack and poked me in the stomach. He seemed to think he had encountered some sea sponge or fungus, and he pulled his finger out with a yell of disgust.

"Let me put it to you blunt," one of the curators said finally. "We always have more material than we can put on display. This one's broken. It's just not worth it. We don't restore found art; it isn't culturally significant. We offered to sell it back to Camptiffler and he said something very rude that I won't repeat. Typical, really. I think the time has come, Gentlemen, Ladies, to put it in the dumpster."

And so I was put in a giant metal chute and sent sliding down three stories, head first, into a metal dumpster at the back of the museum where the leftover fragments of the workroom were usually discarded. When I hit, the stone casing around me exploded like a small bomb into a million pieces, and I lay in the darkness of the evening in a pile of stone and wood and canvas and a cloud of dust.

9

I picked up Venus, shook the rock dust from her, and climbed out of the dumpster. The alley behind the museum was dark and cold and still. The brick wall had a small metal back door, maybe a janitor's entrance. I sat on the low concrete step, stood Venus next to me, and began to pick bits of rock out of my hair. I was thinking.

Was that actually Kitty? I began to doubt myself. I hadn't seen or heard her in years. It wasn't hard to imagine another woman who accidentally had a similar voice. Ah, but it wasn't a similar voice. All the pseudo-Kittys had sounded faintly like her twenty-five-year-old self. But this one was different. It had the same spirit but the surface was aged. Recalling the sound of it sent another shiver through my body. Venus, I'm in the same city as Kitty. What should I do?

I took a breath. My lungs stirred into life for the first time since the magma. It's difficult to breathe magma because it is too viscous. It's also difficult to breathe with a stone strait jacket. But now I felt like I was coming back to life, and I lifted my head and stared around the little alley.

The opposite side was a blank brick wall. One end of the alley was blocked by a rusty old chain-link fence with coils of cyclone wire on top. The other end was open to the street, and the glitter of streetlights and passing headlights partly lit up the space. I noticed, suddenly, that I was not alone. In the shadow of the dumpster, wrapped up in a blanket, a man lay on the blacktop and gravel. He was using a rolled up pair of blue jeans as a pillow. His hair was gray and black in streaks, greasy and long, and his eyes were open. He was watching me solemnly.

When he saw me looking back at him he grinned and sat up, leaning back against the grimy dumpster and pulling the blanket close around himself, tenting it over his shoulders.

"I saw you," he said. He started to laugh in a horrible wheezing rattle. I thought he was going to die. He bent over his lap, his face crunching into a wrinkled ball, coughed, spat something yellow on the blacktop, and then recovered and sat up straight again. "I always wanted to get in there. They got whole rooms with rugs on the walls. Just rugs. I could do with a rug. My blanket is shot." He poked a dirty finger out through a hole in the blanket and wiggled it at me. "Plus they got a fountain. You could get a hundred dollars out of that fountain. It's covered over in change. And they got a cafeteria. Sticky buns in plastic. You know what I mean? You know those sticky buns? I always wished I could get left in there all night. I'd take a few things and get out the back window. But I never could do it. I tried hiding in the bathroom at closing time. But the guards found me and hauled my ass out. That was last year. My clothes, they're a little too dirty now, and I can't even get in the front door. They don't let me in. But holy mother of all tricks, I never thought of dressing up as a statue. That beats all. I never seen anything like it. Hats off to a genius. I mean, if I had a hat." His hand came up with a bit of blanket tented over it and he doffed an imaginary cap. "Crazy. Genius, but crazy. The look on your face when you come climbing up out of the dumpster, it was priceless. You got to be cold. It's forty degrees out and you gone and took off your statue suit."

"I'm not too bad," I said.

"Well," he said, "you can have my extra pants if you like. A guy with imagination like you, I'll share."

"Thanks," I said. I couldn't walk around the city naked. He held out the rolled up pants he had been using as a pillow, and I took them and stepped into them. They were too short and ended halfway down my calves. But they fit all right around the waist.

"You need some fattening up," he said. "What's

that anyway? That a big chocolate bunny?"

"That's Venus," I said.

"It edible?"

"It's iron."

"Hm, supposed to be good for you. Hard on the teeth though. I mean, if you got any." He opened up his mouth wide and showed me his gums. He only had about five teeth left.

"You know where I can get a shirt?" I said.

"Sure," he said. "Right over there. Shirt grand central. You just get yourself over the razor wire and climb up to the open window on the third floor." He nodded to the fenced-off end of the alley. "I'm just kidding," he said. "Don't go hurt yourself. Hey, man, what are you, crazy? Gimme back my pants before you rip 'em all the smithers on that razor wire!"

He had a point. I took off his pants, lay them on the ground at the foot of the fence next to Venus, and began to climb. On the other side, about thirty feet away, the back wall of a department store rose up. The windows on the first floor were barred, but the third floor had an open, dark window.

The man stood up and hobbled over with his blanket still tight around his shoulders. "You really are crazy," he said with a certain admiration, looking up at me as I neared the top of the fence. He added, "Don't leave your nuts behind on the spikes."

I didn't worry about the cyclone wire. It slid over

my skin. I threw my leg over the top of the fence and then dropped down to the other side. The man cackled and did a little dance under his blanket. "You're good, you're real good," he said.

I crossed to the wall and felt for handholds in the brick. I didn't mind climbing. The most difficult aspect of climbing is the fear of falling. Absent that fear, the climbing itself is not difficult. I had only one hand. The other was a blackened stump. But any normal building has irregularities and designs almost as if they were made with a human fly in mind. I had no trouble clawing my way up methodically to the third floor window. Then I wormed my way into the darkness. I was determined to find clothes for myself and for that old man. And, I thought, if I see any sticky buns in plastic, I'll take some of those too.

10

That is how I began my career as a burglar. It was a very lucrative career. I didn't need to eat or drink, which saved me some expense. But that is nothing. I could have eaten all my meals at four-star restaurants. I stole a suit with a stylish cut, because the first priority for a burglar is to put on a respectable front. Then I stole enough cash to rent an apartment. A Manhattan apartment is not cheap, and renting with cash is not normal. But if you wear a suit and a tie, you can get away with almost anything. I tried to open a bank account, but couldn't. I needed an identity for that, and when I tried to use my real name the man behind the counter performed a background check and informed me that I was dead. I didn't want him calling the police. I played it very calm, very nice. I laughed and we shook our heads over the crazy world of computers. I told him I'd straighten it out and come back tomorrow, and then I got out of there. No matter. I didn't need a bank account. The whole city was my bank and if I needed cash I just took it.

I bought a very nice silicon hand that stuck out of my sleeve. I wore it during the day as part of my façade of respectability. At night, though, I left my hand on the dressing table and put on a steel hook that strapped over my forearm and around my elbow with velcro. The hook was good for climbing. It could grip into crevasses that my fingers could never have gotten into.

Any establishment less than four stories above street level was likely to have an alarm system. My specialty, therefore, was four stories and higher. It was nothing for me to climb up twenty stories, clinking bit by bit up the brick or cement or steel side of a skyscraper, until I found an open window and a dark room that looked promising. If there were no open windows, I'd pry one open with the hook.

I wore black clothes and a black ski mask. I didn't wear shoes or gloves—my toes and fingers didn't need the extra protection—but I was careful to paint them black so that nothing would glimmer in the night. The paint washed right off in the shower and was no trouble. I also painted the hook black. Over it all, I wore a black cape. The purpose of the cape was to obscure the outlines of my body. In a cape, I might be mistaken from a distance for a bit of cloth, or a shadow, or some flapping newspaper in the dark. Without the cape, the animal prowl of my limbs might have attracted attention.

I was good at evading the police. The reason is that I could climb anything and was not afraid of falling. Once every three or four months I'd be spotted climbing the side of a building, the call would go out, and the police would converge on the area. Usually by the time they arrived I was gone. Either that or I would climb into some dark crack between two buildings and shake them off my trail.

When I became more famous and the NYPD felt honor bound to kill me, they tried helicopters. The helicopters were even easier to evade. I discovered an excellent ruse one night when three helicopters roared around the corner and shined their spotlights on me. I was fifteen stories up the side of a smooth concrete building. I meant to turn around and wave at the pilots, but I slipped and fell and made a giant pothole in the street below. I wasn't hurt, of course. But the next day the newspaper ran an inch-high banner: "MONKEYMAN'S FALL FROM GRACE." Ironically, the building was called Grace Hall. They thought I was dead. Maybe they thought I was spread around so thinly that there was nothing left to see. Or maybe they thought a pack of dogs had run off with the remains. In any case, I laid low for a while and lived off of my store of cash. When I was spotted again, about half a year later, I became a public hero.

By that time I had a very nice twelfth-story apartment with a balcony overlooking Central Park. Venus, a little blackened and vague in her facial features, stood next to a potted fern. I had a king-sized water bed that I used for meditating when I wasn't burglaring; I didn't need to sleep. I had a flat screen plasma TV in my living room, and I watched myself on America's Most Wanted. They showed actual footage. I looked superb. I was jumping from one building to another, my black cape billowing out behind me, the black steel hook clearly outlined against a large orange moon. Three police officers were scrambling on the ground yelling and pegging at me with their service revolvers. The bullets, of course, bounced off. It was very dangerous work. They could have killed anybody with the ricochet.

11

I had found the apartment building where Kitty lived. She was Kitty Kack, a horrible combination. Dr. Kack was long retired. I wanted to stroll past her building to catch a sight of her, but it hurt my stomach, somehow, to spy on her like that. For all that I was Kwark-Kinged and impervious on the outside, I felt jittery on the inside. Even a glimpse of her bundled in a coat reminded me of all the ways I had failed her. I was also afraid that she might recognize me. I had never meant to come back.

But the thought had a way of creeping into my soul. Sometimes I robbed buildings as far away from her apartment complex as I could get in a night, to avoid temptation. Sometimes temptation got the upper hand and I'd rob the building next door. The brokerage firm on the eighth floor, just across the street from her apartment, had more than its fair share of break-ins. Inevitably, one night around three o'clock, I climbed the side of her own building and hung to the outside of her balcony, my mind in a fire of confusion. She would be asleep, of course. Could it hurt anything to look at her? Just to look at her once and then creep away? I'd promise never to come back.

I vaulted the railing and tiptoed silently among the flowerpots. The door to the balcony was closed and locked but there was an open window beside the door. I sat on the windowsill and looked into the shadowed room. I could see a bed and two long humps stretched out side by side under the comforter. One of the humps was snoring softly. I took off my ski mask, folded it in my lap, and waited with unbearable impatience for my eyes to adjust. After ten minutes I could see the whole room. He was farther from the window, curled on his side, his face buried in the blanket. She was closer to me, lying on her back, her head propped up on the pillow, her eyes wide open. She was looking directly at me, a glitter in her eyes from the light that came in over my shoulder.

"Hello," she said, in her old lady's wobbly Kitty voice. She sounded calm, amused, and friendly. "You do look the same. Funny that I haven't forgotten the details after all these years. Who would have thought?"

She sat up in bed and a bar of light from the window fell across her face. I could see her clearly now. It was absolutely Kitty. She was eighty and I had not seen her face-to-face in fifty-five years. Her frizz of hair was thinned out and gray, more like a delicate halo of moonlight than the electric mane it used to be. It was so thin that I could see through it to the spots of discoloration on her scalp. Her face was as narrow as ever, but etched now with lines. Not harsh or bitter lines but smile lines around the eyes and mouth. She smiled and the loose skin fell into an easy expression of good humor. Her eyes lit up. Under her nightgown her shoulders and chest looked brittle. Her hands, lying on top of each other on the blanket, were translucent skin over thin bones.

"I think it must be the artichoke dip," she said, pleasantly. She spoke with a kind of slowness and precision as if making up for the slight lack of control in her voice. "It makes me dream the strangest things. I don't mind though."

"I thought you'd be asleep," I said in a gasp. "I didn't want to frighten you."

"That's very kind of you," she said. "Not much frightens me at my age, you know. Especially not dreams. And particularly not dreams of old, old friends. You're quite welcome to sit and talk to me." She smiled again.

"You look beautiful," I said. I was dizzy from astonishment. I thought I'd be shaking or sweating or ill from too many knots in my stomach after fifty-five years of dreaming of her, but this was not the case. After the first shock I felt like laughing, like drumming my feet on the floor and shouting out with glory. I didn't, of course, because I didn't want to wake up her husband.

"Thank you for the compliment," she said. "I'm a skinny old witch compared to when you were alive. But I suppose I was a skinny young witch then. I can't get over how you look *exactly* the same."

"Down to the stubble," I said, running a finger over my chin. "It's the Kwark-King, you know. I can't shave because the bristles are indestructible."

"Oh yes, the Kwark-King would do that to you. But you didn't survive it. I can't tell you how bad I felt." She frowned, and her loose old expressive face became sad. "You wanted so much to try it. I suppose you would have died of AIDS anyway. But it was a terrible thing." Then she came back to the present and smiled, her face lighting up. "I'm very glad to see you again."

"I thought about you constantly," I blurted out. "I was under the ocean all those years, dreaming about you. I wished you could have been there. It was all so fantastic. Kitty, I saw a, a shipwreck, and a femur, and a . . . a dead whale, boy, you should have seen the dead whale, it was gross. And I got bitten by a shark."

Kitty's smile became a little lopsided. "It sounds wonderful," she said.

"Does it?" I said eagerly.

"You sound very excited. Not quite the same as the Jonathan I knew. Especially toward the end, you know, you were very quiet. You were very sick."

"I was sarcastic and I was a, I was a Dick, Kitty. I wasn't good to you."

"Oh!" she said, grinning at my language. Kitty was never comfortable with swear words or their cousins. "Now that's a pleasant irony," she said. "I must be going soft in my old age." Then she threw back her head and laughed. "All those years, you know, I wished I could tell you how sorry I was. That's a lot of guilt for someone to carry, although arguably it made me a better person. Now I've dreamt up a version of you that apologizes to *me*. What a delicious fantasy."

"But it isn't a fantasy. I was. . . ."

Kitty shook her head. "Oh, Jonathan, we don't need to argue about who was worse to whom. What was that word you used for me? Flibbertigibbet." She laughed gleefully, putting her skinny old hands over her mouth, looking for an instant like a very young girl in the shape of an old lady. "Such a funny word. Like a little bird flibberting around in the dust. Neither of us was good to the other. You were a jerk. I like to think I've grown up since then, but . . . you never had the chance. That always seemed like a great pity to me."

I smiled at her happily but I didn't reply. There was no point in arguing.

The lump in bed beside her snorted and stirred.

"He won't wake up," she said, fondly. "Stone deaf. He takes his hearing aid out every night."

"Did he ever try the Kwark-King again?" I asked.

"Oh, certainly, many times. But not on a person. I for*bade* it," she said sternly. "When he retired he brought it home and set it up in the library. He's still tinkering with it. Kwark-King 35.9."

"Does it work any better?"

"I don't think so," she said. "All the animals died. Just like you did. Except for the mosquitoes. They were a terrible nuisance. We couldn't kill them. Even if you hit them with a hammer, they would get right back up and try to bite you. We had to catch them in a jar and take them somewhere else, to get them out of the house."

"You can tell him," I said, "that his machine works better than he thinks. He needs to be more patient. You go into a kind of meditative trance, and it might take a decade or two to come out of the trance. I suppose a mosquito isn't a very meditative animal."

"What a beautiful theory," she said. "Thank you. I'll make sure not to tell him. I don't want him trying out any more cats. Right now he's happy testing microbes, trying to invent a harness for immobilizing them." She patted the lump in bed lovingly.

"I'm so sorry," she said. "I would love to talk to you all night, but I am a little tired. It's been . . . *refreshing*." She lay back down again and smiled at me from the shadows on her pillow.

"Kitty," I said, "do you know, I still love you."

"Yes," she said, sleepily, "of course you do. And I love you." She patted the blanket over her stomach. "The artichokes were restless. I think they've settled down for the night."

12

I never visited her again. I didn't want to interfere with the symmetry of that last conversation. Sometimes I lay on my waterbed and went over and over that conversation in my mind.

"Venus," I said, "I'm definitely in love."

"Don't you want to go back and talk to her?" Venus said.

"Yes, of course," I said. "But no, not really. Not yet, anyway. I wish—"

"You wish?"

"I don't know, exactly. I'm pretty well content. I'm Monkeyman, aren't I? I'll be here for a long, long time."

Years later I read about Kitty's death in the obits. She was eighty-seven and had been sick for months with pancreatic cancer.

Her husband was ninety-nine. He apparently suffered from senile dementia and insisted during the funeral, or raved as it were, that he had personally killed her. "She was sick, and I tried. I tried to save her! It was that, or it was nothing. But it didn't work. It aught to have, but it just never does. I don't know why. I can't figure it out." He died several days later of a heart attack, or of grief I suppose. Charitably, grief for her. In my view, grief over the failure of his machine.

They were buried side by side in St. Michael's cemetery.

I visited the cemetery in the middle of the night. As Monkeyman, I had no trouble climbing over the high iron fence. Inside, the place was almost perfectly dark, only the general glow of the city seeping in around the edges, but that was enough for someone used to the pure blackness of the ocean floor. I had a large suitcase and inside, packed in cloth to prevent them from rattling in the night, Venus, a steel chain, several padlocks, and a small shovel. I had to use my fingertips to feel out the names on the tombstones, but I already had a clear idea of where she lay. I had scoped it out during the day.

I put down the suitcase, unlocked it, and took out the shovel. Then I got to work digging her up. The soil was gravely and heavy and the work was difficult. I had to use both my hand and my hook, and to muffle the noise I wrapped the hook in a cloth. Nobody came to stop me.

After a good two hours I had cleared off her coffin and used my hook to pry open the lid. Crouching in the dim light at the bottom of the pit, I saw her lying peacefully with her thin old translucent hands crossed over her chest and her eyes wide open.

Brushing the fallen soil from her cheek gently, I said, "Sorry, Kitty, I need to do one final test." Then rummaging in my shirt pocket I retrieved a pin and poked her on the cheek. I poked her darn hard, and the pin bent. It wouldn't go in. She was pin-impervious.

"Kitty," I said, tossing away the bent pin, "let's skedaddle then, you and I. No, I forget though, you don't like having poets quoted at you. In any case, it's time for us to go. I know a place we can be together, very quiet, very peaceful, where you can think as long as you like before deciding to move a muscle."

THE AUTHOR

Drawing by Wurge

Michael S. A. Graziano, Ph.D., is a professor of Psychology at Princeton University. When not doing research Michael spends his time writing fiction and composing music. He lives in Princeton, N.J. with his family.

ABOUT THE TYPE

This book was set in ITC New Baskerville, a typeface based on the types of John Baskerville (1706-1775), an accomplished writing master and printer from Birmingham, England. The excellent quality of his printing influenced such famous printers as Didot in France and Bodoni in Italy. His fellow Englishmen imitated his types, and in 1768, Isaac Moore punchcut a version of Baskerville's letterforms for the Fry Foundry. Baskerville produced a masterpiece folio Bible for Cambridge University, and today, his types are considered to be fine representations of eighteenth century rationalism and neoclassicism. This ITC New Baskerville was designed by Matthew Carter and John Quaranda in 1978.

Designed by John Taylor-Convery
Composed at JTC Imagineering, Santa Maria, CA